pen pals

Retro Whimsy
Book Four

sabrina cross

*To Dallas,
Thank you for letting me use your name.*

author's note

This is a sentient object romance. Humans will be getting it on with sentient objects. Don't worry, everyone is gleefully consenting.

If you read the last three sentences and think that's not for you, that's okay. There is still time to put this book down and walk away. No one will blame you. It's the sane thing to do.

But if you're going to stick around please be aware of the following: medication induced weight gain, poor self-image, self-directed fat-phobia, body dysphoria, fat shaming, emotional damage, object insertion, magical curse, unsupportive parents, mental health issues.

If you feel I am missing anything please reach out to me at authorsabrinacross@gmail.com and let me know. A complete list can be found at www.sabrinacross.com

one

· · ·

IT WOULDN'T BE a girl's day if there weren't threats of cannibalism. At least, not when I got Aster and Lendy together.

"You promised the last store was the last store," Lendy whined as Aster led the way to the vintage store. "I'm going to start gnawing on your arm if you don't feed me soon."

"I want to see if they have something real quick. Mission, not browsing." It was a lie. In nearly twenty years of friendship, Aster has never once managed to stay focused in a store.

I followed my friends toward the brick building with a sigh. Girl's lunch had turned into a two hour wander and shopping trip. And we still hadn't made it to the restaurant. I could see the awning of the Mexican restaurant calling to me from down the street.

"Get in here, Dallas." Aster shouted from the door of the shop.

With a last, longing look at the restaurant, I followed them inside. I took in the brightly painted window. The name Retro Whimsy with a very seventies looking flower took up most of the glass.

"Two minutes," Aster promised me as I entered the shop. "I just need one thing."

I didn't roll my eyes at her as she and Lendy disappeared into the depths of the store. It took Herculean effort, but I did not roll my eyes. Instead, I headed over to the counter to wait. One of us had to be the voice of reason, and I was hungry enough for it to be me.

"Can I help you?" A bored voice asked from behind me. I pushed straight from the display case and turned around to see the most beautiful woman to ever exist. Tall, curvy, with long black hair and bright blue eyes I wanted to get lost in. I swallowed and shook my head.

"No, thank you. I'm just waiting for my friends." I waved my hand toward the back of the store, where I could hear Aster's voice.

"Okay, well, try not to dirty my glass while you wait."

I pulled away from the glass case and looked for signs of fingerprints or smudges. I hadn't touched it with anything but my back.

There were no marks. The glass was pristine. But that wasn't what caught my attention. It was the vintage fountain pen on a stand. I was something of a pen whore, and recognized the brand immediately. There was a small note card with a price next to it that had my eyes widening.

"Do you have any idea what those are worth?" I asked the woman behind the counter as I eyed the pen.

"Worth is determined by a person's interest. But it's priced accurately." The woman said. Her sea blue eyes seemed to be assessing me before she slid open the display case and removed the sleek black fountain pen from the shelf. She eyed it briefly, turning it over in her hand before holding it out to me.

"Oh, I shouldn't." My fingers itched to touch the pen. The sleek black body was accented with dulled gold. Real gold, if I recalled. It was a thing of beauty. And even at its ridiculously under-priced cost, it was still out of my budget.

"It won't bite." She muttered something that sounded like 'probably' under her breath. I bit back a smile as she held it out to me again.

Unable to help myself, I took it. The barrel was warm from her touch. I removed the cap to view the shiny gold nib beneath.

"There's no ink in it. We cleaned it when we received it. It hasn't been used since." The woman told me with a flick of her long, black hair. "The art supply store two doors down sells a range of ink though. I'm sure they'll have something that works."

"Oh, I couldn't." But I didn't close the pen. And I didn't hand it back. Instead, I started to mentally balance my bank account.

I was still rolling the pen between my fingers when Aster returned. She held up the sock monkey triumphantly.

"Found it!" She said, waving the ugly thing in my face. "I can't believe they had one."

"You starved me for a sock monkey? You already have a sock monkey." Aster was the girl who brought her stuffed animals to college. I was deeply familiar with her sock monkey, Gerard.

"Yes, and Peaches keeps trying to eat him. I'm hoping if I get her one, she'll leave mine alone. What did you find?" She looked at the pen in my hand. "Oh pretty."

I didn't bother to tell Aster getting her rescue

puppy a sock monkey is only more likely to make her think Gerard is a toy. She'd figure it out on her own. Instead, I looked at the pen I was holding and decided, fuck it. It was going home with me.

"We lost Lendy," I said as I handed the pen back to the woman and reached for my bag.

"She found some jelly lamps and got distracted." Aster brushed her pale blond curls from her face and sat the monkey on the counter. I nudged it toward the cashier and handed over my card. "You didn't have to do that."

"You're buying lunch." I said and handed her back the monkey. I was putting my card and the neatly wrapped pen into my bag when Lendy rejoined us. She held a jelly lamp in her hand and grinned.

"I haven't seen one of these in years," The jelly lamp had a rocket shaped base with a glass center. The glass contained light blue water and some sort of gelatinous purple goo that would float about when warmed by the light. They were very stoner chic.

Lendy checked out, a process that took twice the length of mine so the lamp could be safely wrapped up. She hugged her bag to her chest with a grin. "Food now?"

"One more stop," I said to an echo of groans. "I need ink."

two

· · ·

THE BLACK PEN was oddly warm in my hand as I removed it from the bag and dug out the ink. The art store owner talked me into a bright scarlet red and a lovely sapphire and I was uncertain which to use.

"Eenie-meanie-miney," I pointed to the scarlet ink. "Moe. Red it is."

I uncapped the small glass bottle and dipped the nib into the deep red ink. There was a moment of satisfaction as the ink entered the pen through the piston. I filled the pen and wiped the nib off on a paper towel before putting the cap back on the ink.

After putting the inks away in my desk, I found one of my good notebooks. The kind too nice to write in because I could never do them justice. But a good pen deserved nice paper to write on. The black leather bound journal with deckled edges was the perfect companion to the Montnoir pen.

I settled at the counter and picked up the pen. It felt good in my hand. The sleek casing gave way to a 18k gold nib that scratched nicely against the paper as I slowly formed a heart on the page.

Ink flowed as I scrawled out my name. First in print, then in cursive. I didn't know what to write next, so I wrote a curly hello before screwing the lid back on and setting it on the open notebook.

Maybe it would be the combination that helped me get my life in order. They could be the pen and journal I'd been looking for to overcome the executive dysfunction and get organized. I laughed at the fanciful thought as I headed into the bedroom to change into something more comfortable.

———

After a cool shower and a change into pajamas, I returned to the bar to grab my notebook and pen.

I froze when I saw the page. I'd left the journal open on the bar when I'd gone to shower. The page had been mostly blank. Now lines of cramped red writing filled the page.

Hello Dallas, I read before jerking back to look around my apartment. I checked the door, it was locked and the safety chain was engaged. There was no way anyone could have gotten in while I was in the shower. I was on the third floor, and while I had a balcony, it was a fair distance from the neighboring ones.

I checked it anyway and the safety bar my parents' had insisted on was still in place. I was alone in the apartment. That much I was certain of.

Still, I approached the bar with caution. Something weird was going on and I was damned if I ended up in my own true crime podcast episode one day.

"Here lies Dallas, she died because she was too stupid to call the cops when someone was clearly fucking with her." I muttered as I leaned over the journal.

Hello Dallas, I read again before continuing on.

I don't mean to frighten you, though I undoubtedly will. I'd say it's nice to meet you, but we haven't properly been introduced. I am Ryder, your pen. Yes, you read that right.

My gaze flew to the Montnoir pen sitting beside the journal. I couldn't remember if it was in the same place I'd left it. The cap was loosely on, though I thought I'd screwed it tight.

"Ryder?" I asked. There was no reply. Of course there was no reply. Pens didn't talk. Or write by themselves. I went back to the journal.

Assuming you haven't run screaming from the building at this point, I have a request to make of you. Self-writing like this takes great effort and my energy is waning, but I need your assistance.

The Fates have brought us together, and I believe you are the one who might be able to save me from this state.

"The Fates have brought us together?" I laughed at the cheesy line. If a guy at the bar dropped that on me, I'd probably laugh in his face before walking away.

I jumped back as the pen wiggled a little on the bar top. The stool I was sitting on fell to the floor as panic danced up my spine.

"What the fuck?" I yelled at the pen. "What the actual fuck?"

It wiggled a little again but it didn't do anything else. I thought back to the line about self-writing taking too much effort. Could it be real?

"I'm going to be so pissed if someone is fucking with me," I said as I reached for the pen. The lid fell off when I grasped the barrel and I let out a small shriek before I pulled myself together.

It was quite possibly the coolest thing to ever happen in my life and I was acting like a total baby. For as long as I'd been alive, I'd imagined magic was real and fantastic things could happen. And now that they appeared to be happening to me I was acting like a total wimp.

"I don't know how this works," I said to the pen. "I guess we can try this?"

I put the pen to paper and a dot of ink welled up on the page. But nothing out of the usual happened. I loosened my grip a little and suddenly the pen, oddly warm in my hand, started scribbling of its own accord.

Okay, gotta give it the slack to move. Got it.

I slowly moved my hand and the pen across the page, giving it time to form letters, words.

I suppose you don't believe in fate? The pen wrote.

"I mean, not really. Our lives are made entirely of our decisions." The pen began to wiggle again and I moved my hand slowly, letting it write more.

And you never imagined a higher power had control over the rest? How small-minded.

I huffed, insulted. I was constantly being reprimanded for my head being up in the clouds. I just didn't believe my life was out of my control.

"You know what? No, actually, I'm not doing this. I'm not justifying myself to a pen." I set the pen down, closed the journal, and decided to call it a night.

three

· · ·

THE NEXT MORNING, my journal and pen were where I left them. They didn't appear to have moved and there were no new messages on the pages. If not for the words in scarlet ink, I might have believed the whole thing was a dream.

I stood at the counter in my robe with my morning soda and debated what to do. I had two options, really. I could believe I was crazy and check myself into the psych ward or I could believe the pen had a level of sentience. Neither option sounded all that great, but I hated the hospital grippy socks. I was going to believe the pen was sentient.

The next question was, what was I going to do with that knowledge? The pen, Ryder, had said it needed help and wanted me to save them. I didn't have the first clue how to save a person from being a pen.

I could ask him —them? it?— but I was still annoyed about the small minded comment and didn't particularly want to talk directly. Maybe the store would have some idea?

Except, how do you question a store about your

sentient pen without sounding like a crazy person? I finished my soda and decided I would wing it. What was the worst that could happen?

I rinsed my can and tossed it into the recycling before going to change into a pair of leggings and an oversized t-shirt. Then I clipped my hair up, and got my shoes on before returning to the pen on the bar.

It felt weird to toss it into my purse with the other pens and debris. I desperately needed to clean out. It would be suffocating in there. My shirt didn't have a pocket for me to put it in. I had a couple that did, but they didn't fit right anymore. Maybe I could wear one of the plaids unbuttoned over my t-shirt?

I shook my head. The pen had come home in my purse okay, there was no reason it couldn't go back to the store in it. I scooped the pen and journal off the counter and dropped them into my bag before I could think about it too hard.

The trip to Old Town was uneventful and I was lucky enough to find parking in front of the store. I took a second to consider what I was going to say. It's not like I could walk in there and admit the pen was writing me secret messages.

After a couple of minutes, no brilliant ideas came to me. I guessed I was flying by the seat of my pants. It'd worked for me most of my life.

The goth goddess was behind the counter again when I walked in. This time there was another woman with her. This woman was also tall, with brown hair pulled back in a clip. She wore a pair of black dress pants and a white blouse buttoned almost to the top. Compared to the goth goddess with her long black hair and black and red pin-up style halter dress, they couldn't have looked more different, but there was something similar about them at the same time.

"Back again?" The goth goddess drawled with a smirk. Between the two of them, I felt so sloppy. I tried not to let it show as I threw my shoulders back and approached the counter.

"Be nice, Lacey," the preppy looking woman said with a small glare to goth goddess, Lacey. "How can we help you?"

I started rummaging through my purse to find the pen, cursing myself for just tossing it into the bottom of the large messenger bag.

"I bought a fountain pen yesterday," I started as I finally closed my hand around the pen in question.

"I'm sorry, we don't do refunds." The preppy woman said, "All sales are final."

"Oh, no." I pulled the pen free from my bag and we all looked down at the unassuming black casing with the covered gold nib. "I was wondering where you got it."

I forced a little laugh. "I'm kind of a history nerd and am trying to trace the history of the pen. It's… unique."

"It's a pen," Lacey said, clearly bored. How the woman got into customer service, I couldn't begin to guess.

"I'm afraid we don't have much on that pen." The preppy woman said. "I think it came from an estate sale but I couldn't tell you more. Though that one is such a unique item, I'd be willing to make an exception and buy it back."

"Oh," I looked down at the pen, torn. Did I really want to be the one in charge of saving a cursed pen? I could sell it and make it someone else's problem.

"Look, do you want him or not?" Lacey asked. The preppy woman glared at her.

Finally, I tucked the pen into the front of my shirt, slipping the clip over my collar. I wasn't convinced I hadn't gone crazy, but I couldn't leave the pen there. I was already too invested in it. A fact that would probably surprise the pen as much as it surprised me.

"No, sorry. I'm keeping it."

I thanked the women and left the store. It wasn't until I was back in my car and pulling out into traffic that I realized Lacey had called the pen a him.

four

. . .

"THOSE STORE PEOPLE know more than they were willing to tell me," I told the pen, driving home. I had a list of chores I needed to get through that day but they could wait. I couldn't very well go grocery shopping with a cursed pen clipped to my collar.

"Of course they do," a male voice said. I screamed and jerked the wheel. I drove up over the curb before slamming on my breaks and coming to a stop on a usually quiet residential street.

"What the fuck?" I pulled the pen free from my collar and glared at it. "You talk?"

"Well, yeah." The voice had a light accent, something East Coast. "I was trying to avoid causing unwarranted panic."

"And you thought revealing you could talk while I'm fucking driving was the best idea?" I let out a short, humorless laugh and tucked the pen back into my shirt. My pulse had mostly returned to normal. I checked the, thankfully empty, street and pulled back onto the road.

There was a beat of silence before the pen

hummed. "That might have been a miscalculation on my part."

I didn't even know how to respond. Duh felt right. No fucking duh. With a heaping side of what the fuck.

"I apologize for any distress," Ryder, the pen, said.

I made a humming noise but focused on the road instead of the talking pen clipped inside of my shirt. It was warm against my chest as it nestled between my boobs. I tried not to think about the fact there was a man in the pen.

In the pen? Was the pen? So many questions and I didn't have a clue where to start.

"The women who own that store are not what they seem," Ryder continued. "I'm not sure what they are, but there's more to them than they appear."

"Other than being a little rude, they didn't seem all that strange to me." I didn't bring up the fact one of them had called the pen a him and not an it. I couldn't be sure that wasn't me mishearing and I didn't want to sound crazier than I already felt.

I was having a conversation with a pen for fuck's sake.

"Then you weren't paying attention." His voice was derisive and I kind of wanted to hit him. Except he was a pen and tucked between my tits. It would hurt me more than it would hurt him.

"I paid plenty of attention." I shot back. It was a lame shot and we both knew it. But thankfully Ryder had the sense to shut up until we pulled into the parking lot at my apartment building.

"Then you realize she was testing you," Ryder said as I put the car in park, and gathered the contents of my purse from the floor boards where it all fell when I slammed on the brakes.

"Of course I did."

Of course I hadn't. But once Ryder said it, it made a certain kind of sense. Why else offer to buy the pen back thirty seconds after telling me no refunds? And I was more certain Lacey had, in fact, called Ryder a him.

"Lacey knows what you are." I said, curious to see if Ryder would agree.

"They all do." He agreed. "They're up to something but I'm not sure what."

"What does it have to do with you and how you became a pen?" I asked. "Wait no, let me get inside before we talk about this."

I got out of the car with my mind turning over all of the possibilities. Was the pen so cheap because they knew it was cursed and wanted to get rid of it? Had they set me up?

That felt too egotistical. But even as I rejected it, I couldn't help but wonder if it was true.

five

. . .

RYDER and I were silent as we entered the building. I said a quick hello to one of my downstairs neighbors as she exited the elevator before I got on. I should have taken the stairs but I was too tired. I'd take them later.

The trip to the third floor felt terribly long and the silence was awkward. I'd always been pretty good at being with people in silence but something about that one felt heavy.

It was a relief when the elevator doors finally opened on my floor and I could exit into the hallway. There were four units on each floor and I was the farthest from the elevator on the left.

It took me a moment to dig my keys out of my bag — don't ask me why I'd thrown them in there — and get the door unlocked. But finally, Ryder and I were back in my apartment.

"Okay, so talk." I said as soon as the door closed behind me. I dropped my keys and bag on the counter before grabbing a soda from the fridge on my way to the couch.

"The women have nothing to do with my being cursed," Ryder started.

I kicked off my shoes and sat down on the couch. I pulled Ryder free from my shirt and set him down so he was propped up against a pillow. It felt less weird than talking to my tits.

"Okay, but they have something to do with you ending up with me." It was a statement. We'd already established that, kinda.

"Yes. I'm fairly certain the dark haired one changed the price when you came in. I can't be certain that's what she was doing, but contextually it makes the most sense."

I stopped to think about that. What was it she had said? Value was determined by the person but the price was correct? Correct for whom?

"Okay, I'm going to ignore that for now." I popped the tab on my cola.

I waited a second for the fizz to settle before taking a large drink. I'd given up energy drinks a few weeks prior and the diet soda was a poor replacement. It was joyless, but it beat the caffeine withdrawal headaches.

"Tell me about you," I said, eyeing the pen. "How did you end up in a pen? As a pen? I'm not sure how all of this works." I waved my hand at him, gesturing to the whole pen situation.

"As a pen," Ryder confirmed. "I asked the wrong people the wrong questions. Turns out street gangs don't like it when journalists get nosy."

There was a shrug in his voice, like it was nothing. I didn't believe it was so simple but I didn't push him. If he didn't want to go into the details, I wouldn't force them out of him. Not yet.

"How long have you been like this?" I asked instead.

"Since nineteen-twenty-one." He made a small humming sound. "I'm not entirely certain how long ago that was. Time doesn't seem to work the same now."

I slow blink. He'd been a pen for over a hundred years. "It's twenty-twenty-six."

"Oh." And that was all.

The silence was heavy again. Weighted in a way that made me want to break it but I didn't know what to say.

Sorry about the fact you've been a pen for more than a century didn't feel like enough. I wondered what was going through his head. Was the time longer than he thought? Shorter? Was he okay?

Before I could think of something to say that didn't feel incredibly stupid, my phone chimed. I dug it out of my pocket and saw a new message from Aster.

We're going out tonight. I'm picking you up at 6:30. No excuses.

I groaned and tried to think of an argument to get out of it. It wasn't that I didn't want to see Aster. I just really wasn't into going out right now.

"Is everything okay?" Ryder asked, startling me.

"Just peachy."

six

. . .

I SPENT a solid hour trying to come up with excuses to get out of going out with Aster, but she wouldn't hear of it. My best friend was nothing if not determined.

Eventually, I left Ryder alone in my apartment to run my errands. I needed to get groceries and return some books to the library. I'd meant to return the books the day before when we'd all played hooky but I'd forgotten them at home again.

It was after three by the time I made it home, weighed down with grocery bags. Dread pooled in my belly as I took the elevator to the third floor and let myself into the apartment.

"Welcome back," Ryder said from his position on the bar as I dropped everything on the kitchen floor before tossing my bag and keys on the counter.

"Thanks," I said, dropping to a crouch to sort through the bags to find the cold stuff. "I should have left the TV on for you or something. I'm sorry I didn't think of it."

It had to be boring to be a pen. I'd have been raving mad after a hundred years of my own thoughts. I could hardly tolerate thirty minutes of them without seeking distraction.

"It's fine, Dallas. I'm used to the quiet." Ryder's voice was quiet. There was something in it I didn't like.

"When was the last time you talked to someone?" It couldn't have been easy to strike up a conversation when you're stuck as a pen.

"Nineteen-twenty-two. It-it did not go well." He didn't go on and I didn't push. I just put away the cold groceries. Given my reaction, I could imagine well enough how that had gone.

I shoved all of the empty grocery bags into a cabinet under the sink and looked around for a moment before deciding I could leave the dry groceries for later. I needed time to get ready before going out.

"Do you want to watch something while I'm getting ready? Catch up on the news or something?" I felt weird leaving him sitting on the counter with nothing to do.

"It's not necessary."

"Did I ask if it was necessary? I asked if you wanted it." I sighed and grabbed the pen from the counter and took it back into the living room.

I propped Ryder against an empty flower vase on the end table and turned on the TV. I thought for a moment before turning on one of my favorite series about a British crime family during the 1920s. It should be familiar to him.

"You don't have to."

"Shut up and watch the show." I left him there to watch while I went into the bedroom to face my own battles.

Aster hadn't told me what we were doing but for her, out usually meant dinner and a live show or dancing. We weren't in our twenties anymore and didn't tend to close down the cheap bars anymore but the girl liked to dance.

I opened my closet and considered my options. Jeans were out. I didn't have a single pair that fit anymore. It was warm enough for a dress but most of mine we're all tits now.

My nice, dark blue jeggings were clean and still mostly fit so I put those on. I would wear a pair of low-heeled booties and a dressy top and call it a day.

Except none of my nice tops fit. I struggled my way out of the third top I'd tried on and threw it across the room with a frustrated scream. I hated this. Every part of me tingled with rage.

Rage at my body. Rage at my doctor. Rage at Aster for putting me through this, even though she didn't deserve it. I hated everything so much it burned me from the inside out.

"Dallas? Are you okay?" Ryder's voice called from the living room.

I stormed out there in my jeans and a black bra that my boobs were squishing out the top of because even it didn't fit right.

"Do I look okay?" I waved my arms up and down, showing off my stupid, useless body. The one that didn't have enough neurotransmitters in the brain to keep me sane and the one that broke down in the face of medication. The one that decided to gain ten percent of my starting body weight in three months and now wouldn't shed the pounds.

"I'm afraid I don't have a decent way to answer." Ryder's voice was strangled and I realized I probably looked completely deranged standing there in my jeans and bra with my short black hair standing up in multiple directions from pulling the shirt over my head. I was hot and sweaty and shaking with anger.

"Good. Don't answer that." I whirled around to go back into my bedroom to try to find something else.

"Dallas—"

I ignored Ryder and stormed back into my room. In the end, I pulled on a stretchy t-shirt with a rounded hem and low scoop-neck. Hopefully my boobs would be distracting enough to hide the fact that my clothes were absolutely going to be too casual for whatever we were doing.

And if not, fuck them. What did I care?

seven

. . .

"THIS SHOW IS HIGHLY INACCURATE." Ryder said when I came out of the bedroom the next time.

"We don't watch it for accuracy," I said on my way to the kitchen.

"Then why do you watch it?"

"Because the actors are all hot." I move my wallet and the journal from my large messenger bag to a smaller purse. I'd already tucked my lipstick and compact in there so I was pretty much ready to go.

I returned to the living room where the TV was still playing but Ryder didn't seem to be paying attention. I don't know how I knew, but I had the distinct impression he was looking at me.

"Is that what you like?" His voice was genuinely baffled, and it made me laugh. I looked at the TV with the guys in suit pants and sleeves rolled up, slicked back hair, and an air of danger and laughed.

"Not even remotely." I dropped onto the couch and reached for my boots still sitting on the floor under the end table from the last time I wore them.

"Too much drama for me. But they're pretty to look at."

I yanked one boot on and zipped it up while Ryder made a humming sound. I could still feel his focus on me as I leaned forward for the other boot.

"You look nice." I snorted in response.

"You don't have to give me flattery. I realize I was a little crazed earlier. It's fine." I shoved my foot into my boot and yanked the zipper up.

Ryder didn't say anything else. I could feel his focus leave me and I missed it immediately.

We sat in silence for a few minutes, just letting the TV play. The quiet was starting to feel heavy again. I was about to say something, no clue what, when my phone chimed. A text from Aster letting me know she was in the parking lot and she would be up in five minutes if I didn't come down.

"Do you want to come tonight?" I hadn't intended to bring him with me, but I felt weird about leaving him alone in my apartment for some reason. It wasn't like I was going to be able to talk to him when out with my friends.

"Where?"

"I have no clue." I got to my feet and reached for the remote then paused. If he didn't want to come with me, I could leave the TV on for him at the very least. "Or I can turn on something else?"

"Do I have to be in the bag?"

"Well, it's a different one tonight." I held up the smaller purse. "There's a small pen pouch so you won't be rattling around in the bottom."

"I suppose that would be okay."

I couldn't explain the relief that washed over me at his agreement. I turned off the TV, slid Ryder into the pen slot, and grabbed my keys on the way out of the apartment.

I wished I would have driven myself.

The thought danced through my mind as I nursed a drink in the booth at the club. The DJ was decent but too loud and I wasn't in the mood to dance.

I'd appointed myself drink minder and stayed in the booth watching Aster, Lendy, and some of our other friends on the dance floor. At first, Aster had tried to talk me out onto the floor but I wasn't in the mood. Eventually she gave up and agreed having someone watch the drinks wasn't a bad idea.

The club was packed and seating was a premium. I was sure I wasn't winning any points keeping a large booth tied up, but I wasn't going anywhere. Unless it was home.

Eventually, I pulled Ryder from my bag along with the journal. I flipped to a new page and wrote a quick message.

How are you doing?

I scrawled out before releasing my grip on the pen and letting it sit loose in the cradle of my hand.

This music is terrible.

I laughed and looked around to make sure no one noticed. I set Ryder down and pulled my phone out so it could at least look like I was getting amusing text messages.

This is enjoyable for you?

I stopped to think about that. I'd never been the biggest club girl, but once upon a time I'd liked going out and going dancing. I'd enjoyed finding a partner or two to swing me around the floor. Maybe taking someone home for the night.

But that was a different me. A smaller me.

Someone who had clothes that fit and the confidence that went with it.

Sometimes. I thought about it and gave him more. *Once, it was. I don't know. It's not really my thing anymore.*

I held the pen loose but Ryder didn't move for a long moment. I was about to put it down and pick up my phone for some mindless scrolling when it started moving.

I think you're too hard on yourself. There seems to be something stealing your happiness. I don't understand it. You're—

"What's a girl like you doing sitting here all alone?" Someone slid into the booth with me and I slammed my hand down on the journal to cover the words. Ryder and I had wildly different handwriting. It would probably look like some serial killer shit.

I looked up at the generic looking dude who had taken up space on the other side of the booth. He was average in every way. Police could have taken me to a back room to pick him out of a line-up right then and I wouldn't have been able to identify him.

"I like being alone." I flipped the cover of the journal shut and sat Ryder on top. The pen was warm under my hand and I realized it was always warm, even when it shouldn't be. Weird.

"No one likes being alone." Generic Bob said. "How about I buy you a drink and you can tell me about yourself?"

"I have a drink," I picked up my Long Island ice tea and took a sip to prove my point.

"Well, you could buy me a drink," he said, giving me what I think was meant to be a charming smile. "And I can tell you about myself."

The pen vibrated under my hand and I looked down, surprised. It had never done that before.

"Or you could go back to whatever rock you crawled out from under." I said, setting my iced tea back down.

The guy frowned and shoved out of the booth. "No one wants a fat bitch anyway."

I didn't watch him leave. I didn't need to give him the validation. Instead, I slid Ryder and the journal back into my purse and picked up my drink. I was no longer in the mood to talk to a man. Even one trapped inside a pen.

eight

. . .

"ARE YOU SURE YOU'RE OKAY?" Aster asked as she pulled up in front of my building.

"I'm peashy." I told her, digging in my bag for my keys. "I'm sorry."

One Long Island became three over the course of the night. Three very strong drinks. I thought the bartender found me pathetic and gave me a sympathy pour. Because I was drunk. Very, very drunk.

More drunk than I could remember being in a long time. And I hated it. I hated that I let Generic Bob make me feel bad about myself.

"Don't be sorry, be okay." Aster reached over and took my purse from my hands. She dug my keys out and handed both back to me. "Do you want me to walk you up?"

More than anything, I wanted her to come up. I was so tired of being alone. But it was late and Aster still needed to drive across town.

"I'll be okay." I pushed the door open and tried to get out of the car without unbuckling my seatbelt. It jerked me back and I groaned. "I'm a mess."

"A little, yeah. Sure you don't want to talk about

it?" Aster's sympathy was almost too much to take. She didn't understand. How could she?

Aster had always been the perfect one. Skinny and blonde and gorgeous. She couldn't possibly understand what it was like to be the fat, ugly friend.

"Not tonight," I told her, finally getting my seatbelt undone. "Text me when you get home."

"Text me when you get inside." She said as I struggled out of the car and to my feet. "Dallas, I love you. I'm here when you're ready to talk about it."

"I love you, too." And I did. Aster had been my best friend since middle school. We had a lot of history between us. But there were some things even your best friend couldn't understand.

I finally found my balance and closed the door. Aster idled at the curb as I made my way into the building. A part of me was certain she would wait out there until I texted her I was safe in my apartment.

That knowledge spurred me into the building and onto the elevator. There was a brief, concerning moment when the elevator began its ascent, but I made it to my floor in one piece with the contents of my stomach still in place.

The key was tricky. My hands were shaky and I couldn't quite fit it into the lock. I thought about sleeping in the hallway but my neighbors didn't deserve to find me passed out on the carpet. Plus, Aster wouldn't leave until I texted her.

"Okay, Dallas. You can do this." I muttered to myself as I finally got the key into the lock. I stumbled into the dark apartment, barely remembering to grab my keys. I cleared the door enough to close it, and then I sank down onto the cool laminate of the entryway.

I fumbled my phone out of my purse and sent Aster a quick voice memo assuring her I made it safe. She sent me a text to drink some damn water and promised to text when she got home.

"You're not seriously thinking of sleeping there." A voice came from my purse. Right. Ryder. The talking pen.

I so did not need his judgment right then.

"Thinking about it." I said, digging in the bag again for the pen. I tucked it into the collar of my shirt, snuggled between my boobs.

"You'll be miserable in the morning." A dire warning, as though I wasn't already miserable.

Though, he was right. I was too old to be sleeping on the ground. Plus the metal strip thingy that merged the carpet and laminate was digging into my back.

"Do you want to talk about it?"

"Not even a little," I groaned and pushed to a sitting position before rolling over onto my hands and knees so I could push to my feet. The room spun a little but my stomach stayed put.

I stumbled into the kitchen to grab a glass of water and some ibuprofen. I took the pills and drank as much of the water as I could before I headed to bed.

"Why would you listen to anything that flat tire had to say?" I giggled at the insult. Flat tire. Useless. Funny. Ryder was funny.

"You're funny." I told him, falling face first onto my bed. The pen dug into my left boob but I didn't move.

"Not really." His voice was grumpy. "I don't understand why you'd give his words any weight."

"Of course you wouldn't. You're a man." I grumbled. I wanted to fall asleep but my shoes were pinching my feet and I couldn't toe them off which meant I had to sit up.

That seemed like a lot of work. So I rolled over instead and tried to bring my boot to me. Except my belly kept getting in my way and I struggled to find the zipper.

It was pathetic. So fucking pathetic.

I was pathetic.

Eventually, I managed to struggle my boots off. By that time, I was too tired and feeling too pathetic to bother climbing the rest of the way onto the bed. Instead, I just fell asleep halfway on the bed with my feet hanging over the end.

What did it even matter?

nine

. . .

I WOKE to soft scratching on my skin. Gentle lines across the exposed expanse of my belly. It didn't hurt, not exactly. It was mildly pleasant in a way.

"Mmurph," I muttered, trying to pry my eyes open. The scratching didn't stop. I reached a hand up to wipe it away and encountered a warm casing.

"Ryder?" I knew he could move on his own. He'd written that first letter while I was in the shower, after all. But he'd said it took energy.

Why was he writing on me?

"Good morning, doll." I pried my eyes open and reached up to brush my hair out of my face. I felt surprisingly well for how much I'd drank. My mouth was dry and I felt a vague sense of unease but I didn't have the hangover or nausea I'd expected. Winning.

"What are you doing?" I blinked my eyes open again against the blinding light and saw red on my arm. Cramped block lettering traced letters over my skin.

Strong. My left arm said. What?

"Worshiping you." The words don't make sense. Nothing about this makes sense.

I raised my other arm and saw something written there, too.

Lovely is written across my forearm.

"I don't understand." I push up to my elbows and saw red writing across the top of my boobs. Ryder fell to my lap.

"I've come to the conclusion that modern men are idiots. It's clear you can't see yourself clearly. I aim to help with that."

I pick Ryder up and carry him to the mirror over the dresser. I'd kicked my pants off at some point in my sleep and wore the long t-shirt and my underwear. The red was everywhere.

Lush written on my left thigh.

Soft across the curve of my right breast.

Powerful curved over my right knee.

Curvy. Sensual. Capable. Enduring. Sweet. Beautiful.

I didn't know how I had slept through all of the writing. The scratch of the pen still tingled against the curve of my belly. I lifted my shirt to see *worthy* boldly cross my belly.

Tears welled up and my throat clogged. The way the lines traced over my body was beautiful. Full of whirls and curls connecting the words describing me in a way I couldn't see.

"You are the most stunning creature I've ever seen. That you can't see it is a tragedy. There is not a part of your body that isn't lovely."

I used my free hand to trace the letters of lovely across my forearm.

"Why?" I choked out through the knot in my throat.

"Why not?"

I tightened my hand around Ryder. The clip on the cap bit into my skin. I wondered how he'd managed to get the cap from the nip to the other end for a brief moment but he distracted me.

"I heard that man last night." There was gravel in his voice. "He was wrong. His words were meant to make himself feel better by making you feel small. It is a reflection on him, not you."

I knew that. I did. But someone vocalizing it had hurt more than it should. It was a direct shot at something I'd already been struggling with.

"I didn't always look like this," I told Ryder. I removed his cap and replaced it over the nib to keep the pen from drying out.

"Like what?"

"Fat." The word felt bitter on my tongue. I'd spent my entire life making healthy choices, staying active, relying on some damn good genetics. It felt like a personal failing, even when I knew it wasn't.

I traced a line down the inside of my thigh toward my knee and the *powerful* he'd written there.

"You're hardly fat."

It was a lie. Something people said to make fat people feel less bad about being fat. It was also a partial truth.

"Skinny fat, then." I sighed and dropped my hand away from my leg. I still couldn't pry my eyes off my reflection and the scarlet ink spread across my skin.

"That's not a thing."

"It is." I sighed again and dropped it. Because it was hardly the point. "I've always been a little soft. Not like I am now, but curvy. I've never been squishy before."

"Bodies change, that's normal." Ryder warmed in my hand and I wondered how he did it. Another stupid tangent that didn't matter. None of it mattered.

"It's not normal to gain nearly thirty pounds in two months. It's not healthy, it's not comfortable, and it fucks with the head." I finally looked away from myself and the words he'd written, the patterns he'd traced.

"Wonderful modern medicine is supposed to make us better. Help us function. Except, the medication did nothing for me. And now I've got a fun side of body dysphoria." I tossed Ryder onto the bed.

That was not a conversation I wanted to have standing in my underwear. I found a pair of sweatpants in the drawer and tugged them on. Ryder remained silent as I dressed and I didn't know how to read the silence.

"Your worth is not dependent on your size, you know that."

"I guess so." That was the real kicker of it all. I did know better. If it had happened to one of my friends, I would have insisted she was as beautiful as ever and the number on the scale meant nothing.

But I couldn't seem to do it for myself. I couldn't seem to focus on anything but the new stretch marks, the clothes that didn't fit right. I couldn't find joy in a body that wasn't nearly as strong or as capable as it had once been.

"The right man would worship the ground you walk on. You are perfect, at any size."

"Right, because they're lining up." I grabbed my glass from the end table and walked out of the bedroom, leaving Ryder on the bed.

And if I ignored the quietly muttered 'I would' on my way out, well, it was because anything else was insane.

ten

. . .

I LEFT Ryder in the bedroom while I drank my morning soda and tried to process all of the complicated feelings he'd stirred up. He'd made me take a hard look at myself and I didn't like it.

He was right. I was too harsh on myself. The medication the doctor had put me on for my bipolar disorder was known to cause weight gain. A fact I learned, after the fact. None of my habits had changed, and it wasn't my fault. But that didn't stop it from feeling like a personal failing.

The fact my parents had always treated me like my mental health issues could just be willed away didn't help. Honestly, it was no wonder I was such a mess.

I traced my fingers over the *lovely* again. And again as I leaned against my counter. I was being a brat. Ungrateful.

Ryder had done something lovely, wonderful. And I'd repaid him by yelling at him and leaving him alone in the dark bedroom. I didn't know how to handle all of the emotions and chaos running through me.

They were something I'd discuss with my therapist when she got back from her maternity leave. Something I had to work on. But maybe I could work on something else in the meantime.

I rinsed my can and dropped it in the recycling bin before I headed back to the bedroom and the cursed man waiting there.

"I think we should figure out how to break your curse."

The silence was deafening. The words fell like lead between us. I rushed to fill it.

"I mean, maybe you're happy being a pen. I don't know. But I feel like, if you want to, we should try." I shrugged, trying to downplay the emotions running through me.

"Nobody is happy being a pen." Ryder said dryly. "Why would you want to?"

"Because I don't think you deserve to be a pen. It seems pretty miserable. I'm pretty good at research. It's worth a shot, right?"

The silence stretched like taffy. Sticky and heavy. I traced my fingers over the word on my forearm again. Determination settled in my chest. We would break this curse, whether he wanted to or not.

"I wouldn't even know where to start." Ryder said at last. "It's been so long."

Relief flooded me. We could do this. I could help Ryder. And maybe if I focused my energy on helping him, I could stop focusing all of the negative attention on myself.

It would be nice to feel good about myself again.

"Let's start from the beginning." I scooped Ryder off the bed. "Hold on, let me grab something to take notes."

We headed into the living room and I grabbed

my purse off the floor by the door and removed the journal. Of course, there wasn't a pen in there.

"Would it be weird if I used you to take notes?"

"I'm a pen, Dallas. Use me." I barely managed to smother the smirk at his phrasing. My inner teenager wanted to tell him I'd use him, use him hard.

"Okay, thanks," was all I said instead.

Journal and pen in hand, I swung through the kitchen for a bottle of water and another soda. I tucked them under my arm so I could grab my laptop off the bar on my way to the living room. I dumped everything on the couch and started organizing stuff.

"I should get a fancy pen stand." I told Ryder as I propped him against the vase again, using the curve of the fluted vase to hold him in place.

"This works. It's a nice change from laying on my side for so long, honestly."

I thought about that as I set up my laptop and drinks on the coffee table and opened my journal to a new page. A hundred years of laying in storage. He'd probably been thrown in boxes and drawers and abandoned over the years. My heart ached for him.

"Okay, so tell me what happened. You said you were a journalist?"

"Yeah, I was working a story about street gangs in Chicago."

"Like, Al Capone?" He was in Chicago, right?

"He wasn't high on my list." Ryder said dismissively, as though it wasn't objectively cool he was investigating Al Capone. "There were rumors about weird, shady things going down. Demons and devils and magic. I thought it was bunk. Turns out I was wrong."

My first instinct was to call bullshit. Demons and magic weren't real. Except I was talking to a man who was turned into a pen over a hundred years ago. Obviously it was real.

I don't know what it was about that moment, but the reality of it hit me. Magic was real. Like, really real. Everything I thought I knew about the world was suddenly on its ear.

Shoving back the freakout I could feel coming, I focused back in on Ryder.

"Tell me more."

eleven

. . .

"SO, it probably wasn't a demon deal," I said, hours later. "It looks like those mostly backfire on themselves and rarely work out how the summoner wants."

I'd stopped being freaked out by this sort of thing. It was still really weird, but I'd become numb to it. Demons were real. They didn't like being summoned. Sure, totally. Made sense.

"I'm still thinking witches and wizards." Ryder said from his position in my hand. We'd been making a list of possible methods of curses and crossing them off one by one all day.

I sat back and stretched until my vertebrae cracked. I moaned at the release of pressure and leaned back against the couch. Food was becoming a necessity. We'd been so focused on finding the answer I'd forgotten to eat all day. Or even take breaks, aside from grabbing a water or going to the bathroom.

"You're probably right. It makes a certain kind of sense." I sighed and stuck my pen in my mouth so I could pull my hair back into a ponytail. Ryder made a little sound and I realized what I'd done.

I let my hair drop as I pulled the pen from my mouth with an apology. "Sorry, I didn't think about it. I didn't hurt you, did I?"

"No, it didn't hurt." Ryder's voice was strained.

"Okay, good." I rested Ryder against the vase again so I could pull my hair up. "It's a terrible habit. God, I'm hungry. I think I'm going to run out and get something to eat. I don't think I'm up to cooking tonight. I want to get back to this."

I waved my hand at the mess of the table before me. Pages ripped from the journal, empty water bottles, and soda cans littered the surface. My power cord was stretched to the limit trying to reach the outlet.

"Can I come with you?" Ryder asked. Of course he'd want to come with me. I'd never want to be alone again after what he'd been through.

"Sure, let me change real quick." I was still in the t-shirt from the night before and the scarlet writing was very obvious. I knew I'd need to shower it off before work but I was a little sad about the idea.

For hours, Ryder had been amusing me with stories from his life. He was smart, funny, and kind. If I wasn't violently opposed to dating, he was exactly the type of man I'd like to meet.

Just my luck he was a pen.

I changed into a long-sleeve t-shirt and shoved my feet into some slides and called it good enough. Back in the living room, I debated what to do with Ryder. I felt guilty for throwing him into my bag or pockets.

"I still think the idea of mobsters with witches on the payroll kind of ridiculous," I said, picking Ryder up and tucking him into the collar of my shirt. He was warm against my skin, something I found strange but soothing.

"They got rid of me easily enough. Why wouldn't they use every tool available in their pursuit of power?"

"Well, yeah," I threw my messenger bag strap over my head and let it settle on my shoulder. My keys were still on the floor where I'd dropped them the night before. I scooped them up and left the apartment, locking it behind me. "It's more the witches are real part that's throwing me."

I opted to take the stairs, needing to move after sitting for so long. It felt good to get my blood rushing a little bit.

"Yeah, shocked me at first too." Ryder admitted as I rounded the second floor. "Nothing surprises me anymore though."

"That's a little sad." I was a little out of breath as I neared the first floor but still feeling good. "Sometimes surprises are good things."

"You're a lovely surprise." Warmth seeped through me as I hit the ground floor, but I said nothing.

I didn't know what to do with a statement like that.

twelve

. . .

I ATE my pork rolls and fried rice at the coffee table while I researched ways to break a witch's curse. There was a lot of role playing games, video games, and just plain weird—and frankly bad—advice.

"I'm sorry, I refuse to sacrifice any animal. Can't do it." I said, leaning away from the laptop screen.

"Nor would I want you to." Ryder's voice was amused. "Seems messy."

"Speaking of messy. I've got to take a shower and get to bed. It's late and I have to work in the morning." I looked at the once-again messy table and decided to deal with it in the morning.

"Do you want me to turn on the TV out here or set you up somewhere in the bedroom?" I didn't know if Ryder slept and it seemed like a silly question to ask.

"Bedroom, please." Guess he slept.

I set him up on the bedside table against the lamp. I left the lamp on dim and went to take a shower. It took a little while and some scrubbing to get all of the ink off of me.

I was sad to see them go.

It wasn't until I was out of the shower I realized I should have grabbed clothes. I wasn't entirely sure how it worked but I got the distinct impression Ryder could see me.

With a deep breath, I wrapped the towel around as much of my body as I could. There was nowhere to go but through.

I'd run in, grab my clothes, and run back out to get dressed in the safety of the bathroom. Easy.

"Are you trying to kill me?" Ryder asked as soon as I entered the room. I stopped to look at him.

"What do you mean?"

"Woman, you're standing there, dripping wet, wearing a scrap of a towel. I may be stuck in this form, but I'm only a man."

I flushed, heat surging through my body. "I didn't think…" I trailed off, not sure what to say. I didn't think he'd be attracted to me.

I mean, yeah, he did write all those nice things on my body but I didn't think he meant it like that. Although, in hindsight, I wasn't sure how else he could have meant it.

"You didn't think it would be torture to see you all lush and bare? That I wasn't already in Hell from being pressed between those full breasts earlier? That I couldn't still feel the heat of your mouth?"

"No, I—"

"I was prepared to beg you earlier." Ryder cut in. Which was a good thing because I literally had no clue what I was going to say. "Beg you to take me into your mouth again. But you played it off. It was nothing. A terrible habit. But this? This is too much."

I stood in the doorway to my bedroom with my towel clenched in my hand and my heart racing. It'd been so long since I'd felt anything resembling arousal I'd actually started to worry I wasn't capable anymore.

But arousal tingled across my skin at the dark tone of his voice. At the heat in his words. The little devil on my shoulder wanted to see how much I could bother him. How far I could push him.

"Yeah? And how about this?" With a deep breath, I dropped my towel.

"Fucking Hell, woman." Ryder's words shot through me, sending tingles straight to my clit. Oh yeah, I was totally capable of being aroused. I just needed the right person to pull it out of me.

"Problem?" I felt powerful as I crossed the room toward the bed and the pen resting beside it.

"You're killing me," he said on a groan. "A hundred years and this is the worst torture of this curse."

I had thought to tease him more, to make him watch as I touched myself. But my heart broke a little at those words. As did my resolve.

"I want you to touch me." I told him, dropping down onto the bed. "Will you?"

"Please," the word a prayer.

I snatched him off the end table and lay back on the bed. He was warm in my hand, warmer than I'd ever felt him before. I wasn't sure how to go about getting a pen off but I knew how to get myself there and figured I'd take him along for the journey.

"Tell me to stop if you don't like it," I told him, sliding the rounded end of the barrel over my neck and down the curve of my breast. It left a trail of goosebumps in its wake.

"Don't stop." There was command in his voice now. My entire body flushed hot.

I trailed the pen down over my breast before

rolling it back and forth over my nipple. The warmth of the pen sent tingles through me.

"Why are you so warm?" I teased the tip of my nipple with the end of the barrel, flicking it lightly.

"I have no clue. Magic." I switched nipples and brought my free hand up to cup and knead my abandoned breast.

I traced the pen around my areola, shuddering as it puckered up. It was pleasant, but I was starting to want more. I could feel the dampness forming between my legs, the tension coiling in my belly.

"I want you inside me," I told Ryder, running the pen down between my breasts to circle my belly button.

"God yes," Ryder groaned. "Please."

I slid the pen lower, sliding the barrel across my clit a couple of times before going lower to push it inside of me. I was thankful for the screw cap as I caught my fingers on the clip of the pen for a more secure grip.

My pussy clenched on the pen as I slowly moved it in and out of me. It'd been a long while since the last time I'd had sex, and I was so tight. Even the slender size of the pen was enough to stimulate nerve endings.

I moved the pen slowly at first, increasing speed as pleasure tightened my skin and tingled through my nerve endings. Faster and faster, I fucked myself.

There was a soft vibration as I heard Ryder moan inside of me. It was what I needed.

My body tightened as I got close to orgasm. Impossibly, I was going to come using just a pen. I was right on the edge when there was a blinding flash of white light. I released the pen, still inside of me, and covered my eyes with both hands. Something heavy landed on me and the pen in my pussy seemed to grow.

"What the fuck?" I dropped my hands to find a man on top of me. Inside of me. "What the fuck?"

The man scrambled off of me, his cock sliding across every nerve ending and sending me closer to the edge.

"I'm sorry," he said, moving to his haunches. "I'm so sorry. I didn't—"

"Ryder, if you do not finish fucking me I'm going to lose my mind." I arched up toward him, desperate to come. I hadn't gotten this close to orgasm in months and I wanted it. In spite of whatever insanity was going on.

"Dallas, are you—" Red eyebrows furrowed over crystal green eyes.

"Unless you don't want to," I slid a hand down my stomach toward my cunt. I was coming, then I'd worry about the naked man in my bed.

I snorted out a laugh that died in my throat when Ryder looped his arms through my legs and spread me wide for him. And then he was there, sliding back inside. I threw back my head and closed my eyes.

"No, eyes on me." The words came through gritted teeth. I opened my eyes and looked over the man fucking me.

He wasn't terribly tall or terribly broad, but his dark red hair fell over a handsome face with a lush mouth and square jaw. His belly was a little soft, no defined abs but not a lot of extra weight. It wasn't what I expected him to look like, but I couldn't complain. He was hot.

"Never think I don't want to be inside of you." He thrust hard, buried himself deep inside of me. "That I'm not obsessed with you."

"Ryder," I gasped, arching up into him. I was so close. He must have understood because he brought one of my legs up to his shoulder to free his hand. He pressed his thumb to my clit and rubbed sharp little circles in time to his thrusts. My hands flew to the headboard, gripping the metal frame tight as my body coiled.

Closer, closer, closer.

"Come for me, baby doll. Come on my cock. Let me feel you." My eyes shut again as my entire body went tight. My orgasm broke through me. I shook as I fought for control, but there was no controlling it.

Ryder didn't let up. He fucked me harder, faster. Kept playing my clit until the first orgasm rolled into the next.

"Fuck, Dallas, I can't. I'm gonna—fuck." With one final thrust, Ryder went still inside of me. I could feel the heat of his cum as he spurt against my cervix and walls.

I said a quiet thank you to my IUD as I went limp beneath him. After a long moment, Ryder released my legs and helped me slide them down his body before he ranged himself over me, his cock still half hard inside of me.

"I'm going to kiss you now," he warned, giving me time to say no. Something I had no desire to do.

His mouth was hot and soft as he kissed me gently, sweetly. I wrapped my arms up around his shoulders and held him to me. After long moments, he pulled away to look at me with hooded eyes.

"Not how I expected the curse to break," he says, shaking his head.

"At least I didn't have to sacrifice a goat."

He laughed, causing him to move inside of me. He was still half hard and the friction against my sensitive walls made me arch against him and moan.

"You've gotta stop moving like that," he said through gritted teeth. I thought about it for half a second.

"Like this?" I asked, rolling my body beneath his. "Or this?" I wrapped my legs around his hips and pulled him closer.

"You're going to be the death of me," Ryder said as he started to move inside me again.

"But what a way to die."

thirteen

· · ·

EVENTUALLY, we made it out of the bed to clean up. Any hope of sleep disappeared when Ryder transformed, so I made hot chocolates and popcorn and we curled up on the couch together.

I'd call in sick. Lord knows I deserved a sick day after the chaos of the weekend.

"So," Ryder said, reaching out to tuck a loose strand of hair behind my ear. "What now?"

"I don't know," I admitted. My life was kind of a mess and I couldn't imagine him wanting to hitch his fate to mine. He'd spent a hundred years cursed. Why would he want to start his new life over with someone like me?

It wasn't just my weight. It was everything. Most days I was barely keeping it together. My apartment was always a mess, and I was as likely to order take out as I was to cook. Not because I couldn't cook but because I hated doing dishes.

"I guess," I said slowly, "You can stay here until we can figure everything out."

Ryder's hand fell away from my hair and he returned it to his lap. His face was completely neutral and I closed my eyes against it.

"I see," his voice was equally as neutral. "You still don't believe it, do you?"

"Believe what?" I opened my eyes to see him frowning at me.

"How beautiful you are. How much I want you."

My stomach clenched. It wasn't I didn't believe it. It was I couldn't understand it. Why would someone like him want someone like me?

"You've known me for a weekend. You don't know what kind of chaos I am."

"And you don't want to give me the chance to find out."

I threw my hands in the air. "I don't want to fall in love with you only for you to realize I'm too much."

"Oh sweetheart," Ryder pulled me onto his lap and wrapped his arms around me. "I've waited a lifetime for someone like you."

"You're just saying that because I'm the first person deranged enough to fuck a pen and break your curse. You don't want me. You don't even know me."

"Did you ever think the curse broke because of who you are?" He reached up and tangled his fingers in my hair, demanding eye contact. "That a hundred people could have used me but only you were the one who could have broken the curse?"

I shook my head, unwilling to believe that. Unable to.

"A hundred years of being passed around and never once did I feel the connection I feel with you. The women at the store knew I was meant for you. Why can't you believe it?"

Tears fell as I swallowed around the knot in my

throat. It was terrifying, believing this might be real. That he might actually want to be mine.

"I don't know how this works." I admitted. "How any relationship works."

"We'll figure it out." He dropped his forehead to mine and held me close. "It probably won't always be easy, there will be challenges, but we can face them together."

I closed my eyes and let the words soak into me. Together. We could do it together.

"Then stay," I told him. I opened my eyes and met his green ones. "Stay with me."

I wasn't going to think about the challenges we'd face. The fact Ryder didn't technically exist anymore would be a problem, but we'd figure it out later. I could afford the both of us for now.

"I'm yours."

Ryder pressed his lips to mine and I let go of my worries. They'd be there in the morning and I was going to allow myself to enjoy the night.

fourteen

. . .

"WE ARE NOT GOING to result to the black market." Ryder said over his shoulder as he moved around the kitchen. I sat on a bar stool with a glass of wine as I watched him cook. It was one of my favorite parts of the day.

"I mean, it's more like the grey market, really." I argued. "You're going to get bored if you don't find something to do and you can't even volunteer without some kind of identification."

"I'm fine." Ryder insisted, but I knew it was bullshit. He'd spent the last two weeks learning about modern life. He'd had an idea of it from his time as a pen but he didn't have any practical knowledge about how to use the internet or stream a show.

And while he loved all of it, I could see the signs of him getting restless. I wanted him to be able to find something fulfilling. It didn't need to be a paying job, but something to get him out of the house and fill his day.

"Ryder,"

"Dallas, no." He turned to face me, bracing his hands on the bar between us. "I spent my first life fighting against illegal activity. I'm not resorting to it, no matter the benefit."

"Fine," I pouted. "Go ahead and be all moral about it."

"You love my morality," Ryder said, turning back to the stove and the pasta sauce simmering there.

"I just love you," I told him. It wasn't the first time I'd said it, but I still liked the feel of it on my tongue.

Before he could say anything in return, there was a knock on the door. I frowned in it's direction. Ryder half turned to look at me.

"Were you expecting someone?"

"No," I said, sliding off the bar stool. "Everyone I know would text before coming by."

I lifted the security lid and peeked through the hole but there was no one in the hall. I drop the latch and unlocked the deadbolt to open the door.

"Maybe you shouldn't." Ryder said, coming toward me.

"It's fine." I said, opening the door. The hall was empty save for a wooden box, about the size of a shoe box, sitting in front of my door.

I picked it up and brought it into the apartment, locking the door behind me. Ryder and I both stood in the entryway looking down at it.

"Were you expecting anything?" Ryder asked.

I shook my head and carefully opened the lid of the box a crack. Inside seemed to be filled with some sort of paperwork. I dropped the lid and carried the box to the bar.

"I think it's okay," I told him, setting the box down and removing the lid.

On the top of the pile was an identification card

with Ryder's picture and name. But his birthday was only thirty-six years ago. The age he was when he got cursed. I picked it up and held it out to him.

"I don't understand." He took the ID from my hand and ran his thumb over the plastic card.

"Me either," I said, digging deeper into the box. "There's a birth certificate, a bachelor's in journalism degree, and a passport."

"Dallas, tell me you didn't."

"I didn't!" I looked up at him. "I swear. I suggested it, but I honestly wouldn't know where to start looking for something like this."

Beneath a bank book and social security card I found an envelope with the Retro Whimsy logo on the return corner. Curious, I set everything else aside and pulled out the card inside.

Ryder,

Here is everything you need to start fresh. Try not to stick your nose anywhere it doesn't belong. We won't be able to help you again.

Be happy,

Lacey

Ryder, who was reading over my shoulder, shrugged and looked down at the card again. He took it from my hand and read it again before setting it aside.

"I don't understand this," he said, wrapping an arm around my center and resting his chin on my shoulder. "How?"

"Does it matter?" I asked. It was everything we needed for him to start over. "Like you said, maybe the Fates brought us together. Maybe this is just making sure we can live the life you deserved."

"It feels too easy."

I laughed. "Baby, you spent a hundred years as a

pen. Maybe some things can just be easy. Stop questioning it and let's plan how you're going to spend the rest of your life."

"How *we* are going to spend the rest of *our* life."

"Right, our life."

epilogue

· · ·

"YOU TOLD HIM TOO MUCH," Chloe said, glaring at her younger sister. "He's a journalist. He's going to dig and we can't have him figuring it out."

"He's too busy fucking his mate to have time to dig." Lacey said, in typical middle child fashion. She examined her short black nails before meeting her sister's gaze.

"There is no way he'll figure it out. Even after what he knows, mortals never believe in our reality."

"You have to be careful, Lacey."

"I'm tired of being careful. We've been careful for centuries. It's happening, there are two more being freed as we speak. There's no way they will stop us."

"You're certain?" Chloe pressed, "You know what's at stake."

"We all know, Chloe. I get it. Addy gets it. We're going to make sure we succeed." Lacey dropped her defensive posture with a sigh. "I'm sure. Two more. That makes six."

"It's not enough." Chloe pressed.

"I know." Lacey did her best to ignore the feeling of time running out. It was time to get a little reckless.

The consequences of their failure were too high.

about the author

Sabrina Cross (she/her) is a neurospicy 80's baby from the middle of nowhere Michigan, where she still lives with her cat. She came into her monster romance era early when she fell in love with Beast from the 1997's X-Men animated series. After discovering sentient object romance in early 2023, Sabrina decided to embrace what she calls her 'Hold My Beer' style of writing and gave into the lifelong dream of being an author. When not writing weird monster/sentient object smut, Sabrina can be found hanging out on social media (@authorsabrinacross), reading, or hoarding office supplies.

also by sabrina cross

Yarn & Monsters Series

A True Love Spell Gone Wrong...

When four friends perform a true love spell, things go terribly wrong. Now they're locked into a deal with the devil and have only a year to find love and happiness or their souls are destined to face the flames. Armed with a demon guardian; Clover, Jasmine, Fern, and Violet are determined to beat the devil and save themselves. Except, this curse might be the best thing that's ever happened to them.

Corny: A F/F Candy Corn Romance

Snuggle: A M/F Demon Teddy Bear Romance

Tangled: A M/F Friends-To-Lovers Sentient Object Romance

Knotted: A M/F Demon Werewolf Romance

The Cursed Matchmaker Series

Never Piss off a witch. Or else you may find yourself trapped in a glory hole booth at an upscale sex club. But when the perfect couples hook up anonymously, Josh has no choice but to speak out and help them find love.

The Glory Whole Package

The Glory Whole Experiment

The Glory Whole Redemption

Retro Whimsy Series

Welcome to Retro Whimsy where nothing is as it seems and the owners know just what you need.

Getting Railed

Trogg Trouble

Game Girl

Ghostlight Falls - Shared World Series

Cooking Up A Demon

Planet WLN269 Needs Women - Shared World Series

Taken in by the Aliens

Much Ado About Rutting

Stand Alone Monster Romance

Christmas with the Monster

Can't Yeti Enough

Stand Alone Sentient Object Romance

Light Me Up

Pounded by the Pommel Horse

Sentient Pen15 from Outer Space

Knotty Broomsticks